To Rahila, Akbar, and Zaman—A.M.

For Trevor and Minty—N.S.

Have You Seen Chester?
Text copyright © 2008 by Andrew Murray
Illustrations copyright © 2008 by Nicola Slater

This book was previously published by Macmillan Children's Books
in the United Kingdom in 2008 as *Have You Seen Elvis?*

Printed in Belgium
Library of Congress Cataloging-in-Publication Data is available.

1 3 5 7 9 8 6 4 2   ✦   First US Edition

ANDREW MURRAY

Have You Seen Chester?

Illustrated by NICOLA SLATER

HARPERCOLLINS PUBLISHERS

Buddy the dog and Chester the cat were

ALWAYS
FIGHTING.

Whenever Buddy was eating, Chester would pounce, with a MMMMMEEOUWWWW RRRAAAOUWWWW and a scratch of his claws.

Whenever Chester was sleeping, Buddy would pounce with a WOAH WOAH WOAH and a snap of his jaws.

and they
FOUGHT
and FOUGHT
and FOUGHT.

"This fighting is wearing me out," grumbled Chester.
"I'VE HAD ENOUGH."

And that evening he crept out through the
cat-flap . . . and didn't come back.

When Chester still wasn't back the next morning,
Lucy searched all through the house and all around the garden.

the
washing machine

the
garbage can

the
laundry
basket

the bushes

the
hat stand

SHE LOOKED
EVERYWHERE!

"Perhaps he'll
turn up when
he's hungry,"
she thought.

So she put out a big
saucer of Chester's
favorite fish.
But still Chester didn't
come back.

Lucy made posters
and put them up
all over town.

She asked the neighbors
if they'd seen Chester,
but no one had.

Poor Lucy was very upset. Her eyes were all red and puffy from crying. Buddy felt guilty.

Buddy tried to comfort Lucy. He put his paw on her lap and licked her hand. But she shooed him away.

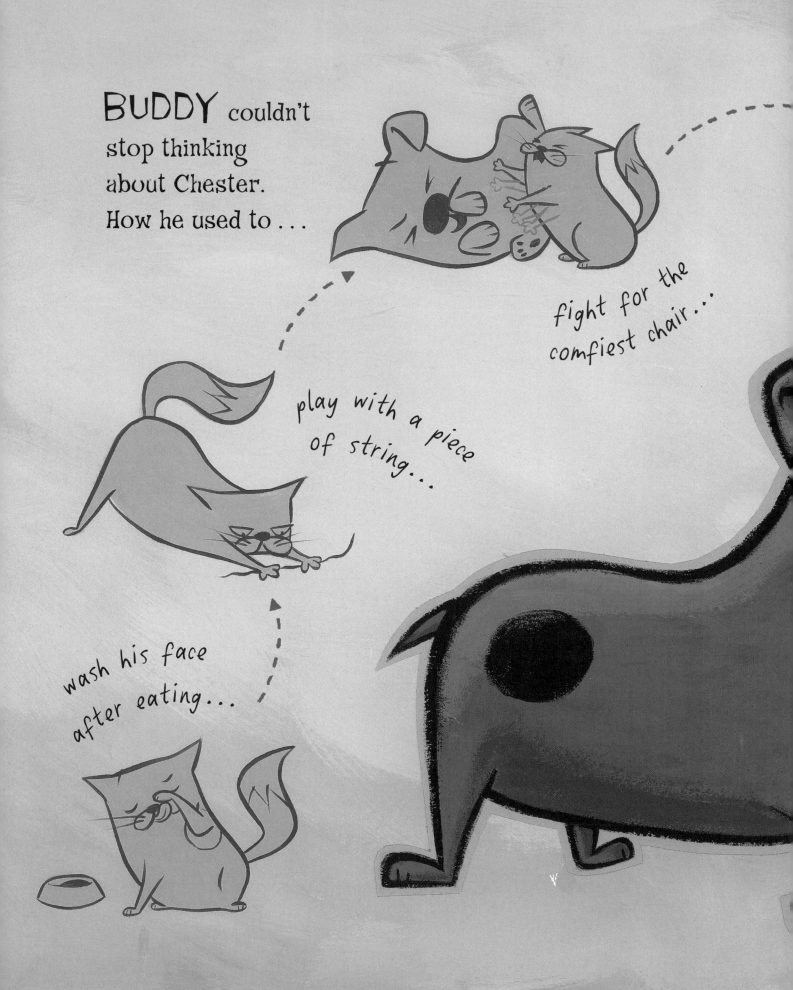

BUDDY couldn't stop thinking about Chester. How he used to . . .

fight for the comfiest chair...

play with a piece of string...

wash his face after eating...

sleep on top of
the television...

I can't believe it.
I think I miss him.

That night
when Lucy had gone to bed,
BUDDY squeezed
through the cat-flap and sat
out into the darkness.

NIGHT!
It was a
cat's world
all right.

Buddy soon realized he wasn't alone.
Alley cats were all around him,
hissing and spitting.

"Stupid dog," they hissed.
"You don't belong here. This is
the night, and it belongs to us."
Closer they came, closer
and closer . . .

"Wait!"
said Buddy.
"I don't want any trouble.
I'm just looking for a . . . a *friend*. His name is Chester."
The alley cats stopped. "Chester?" they said, surprised.
"You're a friend of Chester's?"
"Yes," said Buddy. "He's missing,
and we're worried about him . . ."

"WELL, WHY DIDN'T YOU SAY SO?"

The cats laughed.

"Chester is a friend of ours, too.
Come on, we'll help you find him."

Buddy and the alley cats searched through the night. They looked under bushes and cars, on rooftops, in trees, and in all the gardens and streets and alleys.

By dawn they were
exhausted.
"Oh, dear." Buddy sighed.
"Where can Chester be?"
Just then, there was
a gust
of wind.

Buddy lifted his nose.
He sniffed.
He could smell something.
Something that reminded him of . . .

CHESTER!

"**LEAVE ME ALONE,**"
said Chester.
"I don't want to fight anymore."

"I haven't come to **FIGHT** with you, Chester," said Buddy.
"It's just . . . Lucy's worried about you and, well . . .
I was worried, too.

"Please come
home."

Chester looked at
him suspiciously.

"Don't worry, Chester," called the alley cats.
"YOU CAN TRUST HIM!"

So BUDDY and CHESTER
went home.

"CHESTER, YOU'RE BACK!" shouted Lucy.
She kissed and petted him. And she gave Buddy a big hug.
"Now . . . " she said, "I'm going to get us all some breakfast.
Can I leave you alone for one minute, without you two fighting?"

Lucy came out of the kitchen with lots
of toast, fish, and doggie chews.

"Breakfast!" she called.
But there was no reply.

She peeped around the door and smiled.

"I don't think I need to worry anymore."